DISCARD

The Child's World®

Published in the United States of America by The Child's World®
1980 Lookout Drive • Mankato, MN 56003-1705
800-599-READ • www.childsworld.com

ACKNOWLEDGMENTS
The Child's World®: Mary Berendes, Publishing Director
The Design Lab: Kathleen Petelinsek, Design and Page Production
Literacy Consultants: Cecilia Minden, PhD, and Joanne Meier, PhD

LIBRARY OF CONGRESS
CATALOGING-IN-PUBLICATION DATA
Moncure, Jane Belk.
  My "e" sound box / by Jane Belk Moncure ;
illustrated by Rebecca Thornburgh.
    p. cm. — (Sound box books)
  Summary: "Little e has an adventure with items beginning
with his letter's sound, such as eggs, elves, and an elephant."—
Provided by publisher.
  ISBN 978-1-60253-145-1 (library bound : alk. paper)
  [1. Alphabet.] I. Thornburgh, Rebecca McKillip, ill. II. Title. III.
Series.
  PZ7.M739eMy 2009
  [E]–dc22   2008033161

A NOTE TO PARENTS AND EDUCATORS:

Magic moon machines and five fat frogs are just a few of the fun things you can share with children by reading books with them. Reading aloud helps children in so many ways! It introduces them to new words, motivates them to develop their own reading skills, and expands their attention span and listening abilities. So it's important to find time each day to share a book or two . . . or three!

As you read with young children, you can help develop their understanding of how print works by talking about the parts of the book—the cover, the title, the illustrations, and the words that tell the story. As you read, use your finger to point to each word, modeling a gentle sweep from left to right.

Simple word games help develop important prereading skills, including an understanding of rhyme and alliteration (when words share the same beginning sound, such as "six" and "sand"). Try playing with words from a book you've just shared: "What other words start with the same sound as moon?" "Cat and hat, do those words rhyme?" The possibilities are endless—and so are the rewards!

My "e" Sound Box®

(This book concentrates on the short "e" sound in the story line. Words beginning with the long "e" sound are included at the end of the book.)

WRITTEN BY JANE BELK MONCURE

ILLUSTRATED BY REBECCA THORNBURGH

Little had a box. "I will find things that begin with my **e** sound," he said. "I will put them into my sound box."

Little found eggs.

He found lots and lots of eggs.

Did he put the eggs into his

box? He did.

Little found elves.

The elves danced and danced.

Did Little put the elves into

the box with the eggs? He did.

The elves played with the eggs.

"Be careful, elves," said Little .

Now the box was heavy.

So Little found an elephant.

"Hop on!" said the elephant.

The elephant went up and down.

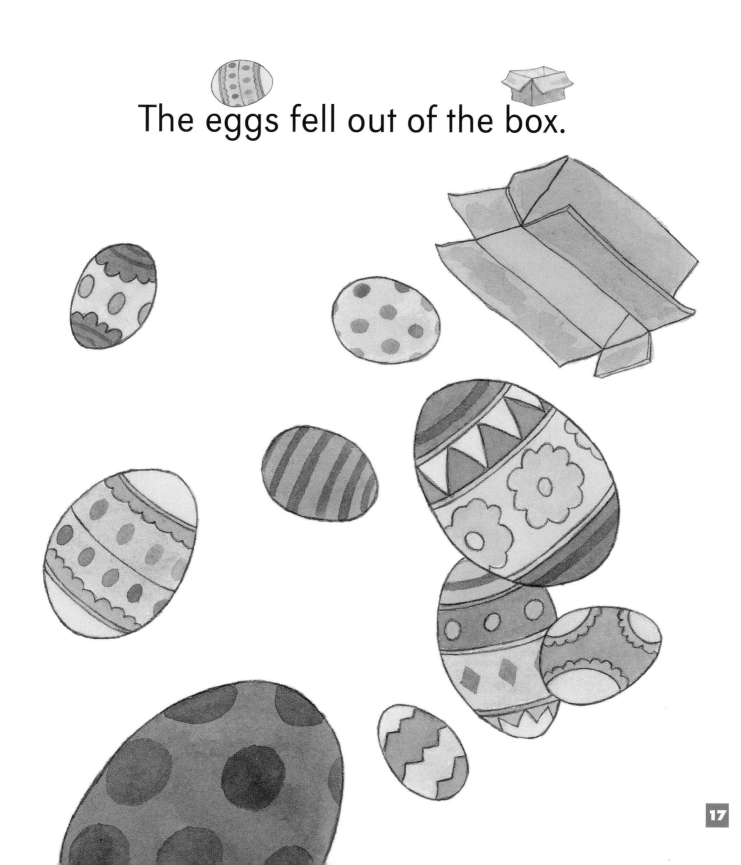

The eggs fell out of the box.

The elves fell, too. So did Little .

"That was a bad bump!" he said.

"What a mess!" said Little .

"Now who will help me fill my box?"

An Eskimo came by.

"I will help you fill your box," said

the Eskimo.

"I know where we can find lots of 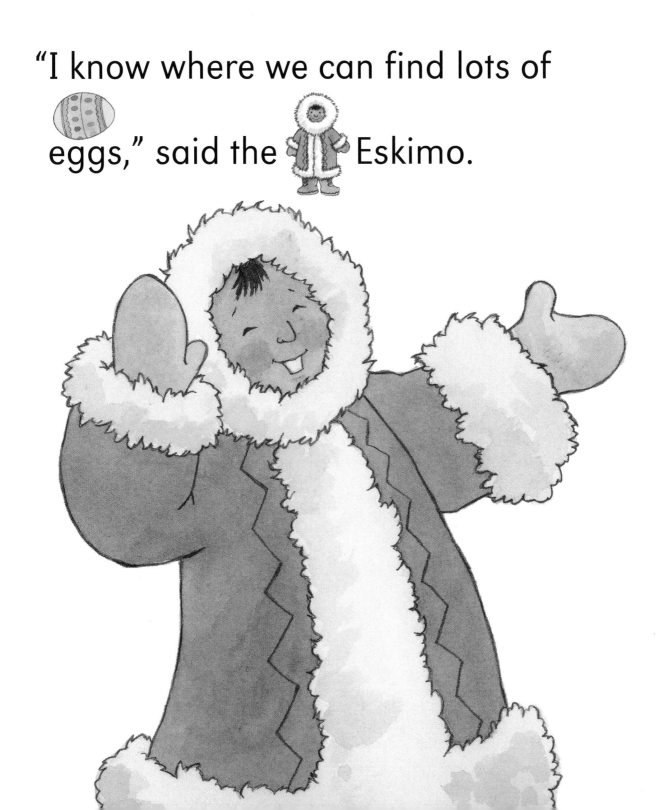 eggs," said the Eskimo.

Guess who had eggs for Little ?

Guess who had pretty eggs for everyone?

Little 's Word List

egg

elephant

elves

Eskimo

Other Words with the Short "e" Sound

eggplant

elbow

elevator

elk

engine

envelope

Words with the Long "e" Sound

Little "e" has another sound in some words. He says his name, "e."
Can you read these words? Listen for Little "e's" name.

eagle

ear

Easter

eel

emu

eraser

More to Do!

Little asked an elephant to help him carry his box of eggs and elves. Elephants are very big. Elves are very small. Can you answer these puzzles about elves and elephants?

Puzzles:

Eddie Elephant is 9 feet tall. Ellie Elf is 2 feet tall. Which one is taller? How much taller?

Answer: Eddie Elephant is 7 feet taller.

Eddie Elephant weighs 8,040 pounds. Ellie Elf weighs 40 pounds. Who weighs less? How much less?

Answer: Ellie Elf weighs 8,000 pounds less.

Here are some silly riddles about elves and elephants!

Riddles:

What weighs 8,000 pounds and wears glass slippers?
Answer: Cinderelephant.

What's the first thing elves learn in school?
Answer: The "elf"-abet.

How do you know there are three elephants in your refrigerator?
Answer: The door won't close!

How many elves does it take to change a lightbulb?
Answer: Ten! One to change the lightbulb and nine to stand on each other's shoulders!

What do elephants do for fun?
Answer: Watch "ele"-vision.

What kind of bread do elves make sandwiches with?
Answer: Shortbread.

About the Author

Best-selling author Jane Belk Moncure has written over 300 books throughout her teaching and writing career. After earning a Master's degree in Early Childhood Education from Columbia University, she became one of the pioneers in that field. In 1956, she helped form the Virginia Association for Early Childhood Education, which established the first statewide standards for teachers of young children.

Inspired by her work in the classroom, Mrs. Moncure's books have become standards in primary education, and her name is recognized across the country. Her success is reflected not only in her books' popularity with parents, children, and educators, but also by numerous awards, including the 1984 C. S. Lewis Gold Medal Award.

About the Illustrator

Rebecca Thornburgh lives in a pleasantly spooky old house in Philadelphia. If she's not at her drawing table, she's reading—or singing with her band, called Reckless Amateurs. Rebecca has one husband, two daughters, and two silly dogs.